3 1192 00242 3539

D0983532

5—

battle : a

miss Bianca story /

FEB 23 1979

BOOKS BY MARGERY SHARP

Bernard into Battle

Bernard into Battle

A Miss Bianca Story

Margery Sharp

Illustrations by Leslie Morrill

EVANSTON PUBLIC LIBRARY
CHILDREN'S DEPARTMENT
1703 ORRINGTON AVENUE
EVANSTON, ILLINOIS 60201

Little, Brown and Company
Boston   Toronto

COPYRIGHT © 1978 BY MARGERY SHARP

Illustrations copyright © 1978
by Little, Brown and Company, Inc.

ALL RIGHTS RESERVED. NO PART OF THIS BOOK MAY BE
REPRODUCED IN ANY FORM OR BY ANY ELECTRONIC OR
MECHANICAL MEANS INCLUDING INFORMATION STORAGE
AND RETRIEVAL SYSTEMS WITHOUT PERMISSION IN WRIT-
ING FROM THE PUBLISHER, EXCEPT BY A REVIEWER WHO
MAY QUOTE BRIEF PASSAGES IN A REVIEW.

FIRST AMERICAN EDITION

LIBRARY OF CONGRESS CATALOGING IN PUBLICATION DATA

Sharp, Margery, 1905–
  Bernard into battle.

  SUMMARY: Miss Bianca's faithful lieutenant, Bernard,
directs a hazardous operation that repulses the army of
rats infesting the regions under the Ambassador's cellar.
  [1. Mice—Fiction] I. Morrill, Leslie H.
II. Title.
PZ7.S5315Bc   [Fic]   78–11332
ISBN 0–316–78326–9

PRINTED IN THE UNITED STATES OF AMERICA

Bernard into Battle

1

The Lull before the Storm

EVER SINCE HE came back from rescuing Miss Thomasina (heiress to the Three Rivers Estate and now happily married to an air-pilot) out of the hands of bandits in the Wolf Range, Bernard had been feeling rather restless. His duties as Secretary of the Mouse Prisoners' Aid Society made almost a full-time occupation, and his leisure was agreeably passed sticking stamps into his album and visiting Miss Bianca (ex–Madam President of the same world-famous organization), each evening from five to six at her Porcelain Pagoda; but Bernard was still restless. Like Alexander the Great, he found himself yearning for fresh worlds to conquer, or at least for fresh adventures.

It wasn't so much the glory he was after, as an opportunity to stretch his new-found capabilities. On previous daring rescues, in company with Miss Bianca, he'd always rather played second fiddle, and having for once had a solo part, longed to perform again. So Bernard sometimes sighed, and one evening sighed at five-fifteen.

"My dear Bernard," probed Miss Bianca gently, "won't you tell me what is on your mind?—or rather you needn't tell me, for I can guess! It *is* dull to return to the daily round, the common task!"

"You've got it," said Bernard.

"I used to feel so myself," sympathized Miss Bianca. "After facing jailers and bloodhounds, how boring it was just to sit helping the Boy with his lessons in the peace and safety of the Embassy schoolroom!"

It was in the Embassy schoolroom that her Porcelain Pagoda was situated, inside a great gilded bird-cage so large (it had once housed parakeets), that there was room for a little pleasure garden as well, with swings and hammocks and a Venetian glass fountain. The Boy was the Ambassador's son, so the Ambassadress was of course his mother, and both thoroughly approved of his intimacy with Miss Bianca, without whom sitting on his shoulder he'd never have attended to his

4

lessons at all! She was a white mouse of excep-
tional beauty, with fur like ermine and eyes like
topazes; the silver chain she wore about her neck
(actually a gift from the Ambassadress) merely
seemed appropriate to her slender loveliness, didn't
enhance it. Bernard for his part was thickset and
a nondescript brown. *His* only claim to hand-
someness lay in his whiskers, which though a bit
short were uncommonly strong.

"I'm sure peace and safety is the best thing for
you," now said Bernard warmly. "You've done
quite enough adventuring!"

"I almost believe I have," acknowledged Miss
Bianca, sighing in turn. "Whereas you, my dear
Bernard, are still in the prime of life!"

"I shan't be much longer," said Bernard gloom-
ily. "So I suppose it's peace and safety for me
too. . . ."

Little did either guess that within a matter of
days peace and safety would be the *last* things to
characterize the Embassy!

"And now I'm afraid it's going to be duller for
you than ever," went on Bernard (little guessing!),
"with everyone away."

For only a few days previously the Ambassador
had taken his family, and most of the Embassy
staff as well, for a month's holiday to a house he

had in the country, where he could relax from being constantly diplomatic, and his wife from her constant entertaining of other diplomats.

"I'm only surprised the Boy didn't take you with him," added Bernard, "as he did to that mountain resort after he had mumps. He's never left you behind before."

This was perhaps a little tactless of Bernard, especially as the Ambassadress had taken *her* quite new favorite, a beautiful white Persian cat named Omar, actually bought to replace Miss Bianca's old friend Shah, now alas no more. But Miss Bianca only smiled.

"The Boy is just as attached to me as ever," said she, "but as he grows bigger naturally needs me less. In the country he will find companions more his own size, that he can play football with!"

It was true, the Boy *did* need her less. Taken off to the country he was particularly sorry to miss a Dog Show just about to take place, for he'd hoped to persuade his mother to buy him a puppy at it. The only dog on the Embassy staff was an old pointer of the Ambassador's, kept always in the country, and the Boy very much wanted one of his own. It was part of his growing bigger: as he wanted to play football instead of rounders, so he wanted, besides even so beautiful and accomplished a mouse as Miss Bianca for a pet, a puppy-dog. He'd even chosen a name—Tinker. But when the Ambassador needed a holiday all other considerations went by the board, and the Boy's constant references to the coming Dog Show had fallen on deaf ears.

For all her philosophy, however, Miss Bianca had indeed felt a pang at the moment of parting, and as usual consoled herself by composing a poem.

BRIEF BUT HEARTFELT POEM COMPOSED BY
MISS BIANCA WHILE THE LUGGAGE (INCLUDING
OMAR IN A CAT-BASKET) WAS BEING LOADED
INTO THE AMBASSADORIAL ROLLS-ROYCE
Go, go, dear Boy, to sport midst rural scenes!
To kick the ball, or head it from the net!

(Miss Bianca was never quite clear about the opposing roles of center-forward and goal-keeper.)

Companion of your youth was I, but now you're
so much bigger,
How natural your need to cut a bigger figure!

She herself was far from satisfied with this poem—*bigger* and *figure* being a false rhyme— but as she murmured it into the Boy's ear on the Embassy steps, he at least found no fault with it.

"Thank you, Miss Bianca!" murmured he back. "You're always so understanding!—and I've told

7

8

Thomas Footman specially to remember your cream cheese!"

Thomas Footman was the only member of the Embassy staff left behind (except for an old night-watchman so very old that everyone knew him as Methuselah), to take care of the Embassy in the Ambassador's absence. As the Ambassadress often said, her husband was far too trusting!—and so it turned out, for Thomas Footman immediately went off home on holiday, leaving Methuselah to manage as best he could—and who possibly might have managed well enough, if he hadn't found the key to the wine cellar and tippled port all day long! Little *he* noticed if anything was amiss; for instance, the very next morning after the Ambassador's departure, workmen from the Waterworks Board came to inspect the big main drain that ran deep below the Embassy foundations, and after descending into it by way of a man-hole in the cellar floor, when they came up again care-lessly omitted to replace the big iron cover prop-erly flush but left it cocked up several inches, so that anyone could have tripped and broken an ankle. Methuselah never noticed. He had an eye for nothing in the cellar except where the port was kept!

Which in a way was just as well, as otherwise he might have had the curiosity to examine a great old claret cask the mice had turned into the head-

quarters of the M.P.A.S.—their Moot House—
and had his eye lighted on the neat match-box
benches inside, and the platform for the Committee ranged with walnut shell arm-chairs, and the
oil painting that hung behind, of a mouse freeing
a lion from a net, he'd have been so amazed he
might have had a heart attack, or if he'd probed
further been asphyxiated, for among the other
treasures the Moot House contained was a slab
of Gorgonzola cheese, brought there to provide
light refreshment after meetings, and now so
powerfully odorous the mice had had to store it
in the hollow under the platform lest its fumes
should overcome them in the middle of Unfinished
Business. As it was, however, only Bernard, pay-
ing a routine visit of inspection to see the Moot
House was kept properly swept and polished,
noticed the cocked-up man-hole cover. It was
really he, not Methuselah, the Ambassador should
have left in charge!

An even graver dereliction of duty on the part
of Thomas Footman was that he completely for-
got about Miss Bianca's cream cheese. However,
Bernard knew his way round the store rooms of
old, for though he presently occupied one of the
best mouse-addresses going (a flat in the Ambassador's cigar-cabinet, after the Ambassador gave
up smoking), he'd actually started his now dis-

tinguished career as a mere pantry-mouse, and in this emergency nothing gave him greater pleasure than to keep Miss Bianca's silver bonbon dish daily filled from the left-behind stock of Camembert. It gave him an excuse to visit her every morning, besides between five and six. No blame could attach to the housemaids, since they'd been taken to the country too, but the store of old tea-leaves they kept for brushing carpets lay untouched and began to desiccate, for no one brushed the carpet even in the Ambassadress's boudoir any more. Miss Bianca did her best there by daily dusting the mantelpiece—and no duster was ever so delicate as the flick of Miss Bianca's tail!—but otherwise the whole Embassy began to get shabbier and shabbier, and quite unlike its old spotless self.

Not that the mice cared. They now had the run of the place quite to themselves, and for days had been scampering through the big stately rooms and sliding (the younger among them) down the banister of the grand staircase, and in general making such whoopee as they'd never been able to make before! There was plenty to eat, even without the left-overs from the Ambassadress's cocktail and dinner parties, for all fathers of families knew their way about the store rooms almost as well as Bernard did, and in fact they too were having the time of their lives!

So it was all the more creditable to one and all that when disaster struck, none failed in duty!

But it hadn't struck just yet, and Bernard's and Miss Bianca's rather sad conversation was interrupted only by a big lion-colored paw patting at the Pagoda's gilded railings. . . .

2
Danger Signals

NEITHER BERNARD nor Miss Bianca flinched, however: 'twas the paw of Algernon, the teddy bear who'd so gallantly accompanied Bernard into the Wolf Range (though but in the role of squire to Bernard's Knight Errant), and who now spent most of his time at his Club in the Boy's play-box.

It was the most exclusive of Clubs, so strictly for Soft Toys that that there was only one other member, also a teddy bear, named Nigel, who'd been given to the Boy so long ago that he now ranked as the play-box's senior citizen. There were besides in the play-box all sorts of discarded games such as tiddlywinks and snakes-and-ladders at which Algernon and Nigel sometimes played—

that is at tiddlywinks, because the snakes com-
plained of the dice hitting their heads or tails:
they'd had quite enough of *that,* they said, while
the Boy still played at snakes-and-ladders! So now
they just lolled about the board treating the ladders
as so many deck chairs, which Algernon and Nigel
thought very selfish of them. However they were
all properly respectful to their betters, and even
the very biggest snake of all, by name Khalil,
whose twelve inches traversed the board from bottom to top, and who was inclined to be a bully,
never failed to hiss politely.

It was a sort of society quite foreign to Miss
Bianca, but she readily admitted that if that were
the sort of society Algernon liked, he had every
right to it, and indeed felt quite flattered when he
left it to visit the Porcelain Pagoda.

"How sorry I am I can't ask you in!" she now
exclaimed.

Naturally she couldn't ask Algernon in; he was
too big to squeeze between the railings. But
through them he kissed her hand, he being almost
as great an admirer of Miss Bianca as was Bernard.

"Now you must give us all the gossip from the
Club," continued she, "you who live so much
more worldly a life than Bernard and myself!
We were just lamenting the lack of all excitement!"

"Well, I don't know that anything particularly

exciting's happened," said Algernon regretfully, "unless you count seeing a rat nosing round the play-box. . . ."

He created more of a sensation than he'd expected.

"A rat?" exclaimed Miss Bianca. "In the Boy's bedroom?"

"A rat!" echoed Bernard. *"Upstairs?"*

"He didn't stay long," reassured Algernon. "As soon as Khalil put his nose out he was gone before you could say rodent. The only other thing I can think of to amuse you, Miss Bianca, is that Nigel's trying to grow a moustache."

"At his age? Still, give him my very best wishes for it," said Miss Bianca, "and may I recommend a touch of Pomade Divine, such as the Ambassador always uses?"

"And which you'll find on the bottom shelf of his medicine-chest," added Bernard.

Whereupon Algernon, who by now had grown quite fond of his aged fellow Clubman, hurried off to advise this treatment, and Bernard and Miss Bianca were again alone.

"A rat!" repeated she. "In the Boy's bedroom! However could one get into the Embassy at all?"

Bernard pulled his whiskers.

"Well, I didn't tell you," said he, "but the Waterboard workmen who came to look at the main drain left the man-hole cover not quite properly replaced; so I dare say *one* rat could get in from the sewers. But since Khalil saw him off in double-quick time, I don't think we need fear any *invasion* by rats—or it might well be the Radish Patch for all of us!"

The Radish Patch was a plot of ground just outside the schoolroom window where the Boy had once tried to grow radishes, hence its name, but he soon tired of gardening and it became a last resting place for fallen nestlings. The Boy, like his father, had the kindest heart in the world, and couldn't bear to see the pathetic unfledged little bundles lie exposed to the elements afresh, so he buried them. He also buried several bumblebees, a tortoise who'd died of old age, and once even a young hedgehog; and thus Bernard, referring to the Radish Patch, was referring to a cemetery, and Miss Bianca barely controlled a shudder—seeing which Bernard hastened to add that he must have eaten something that disagreed with him for lunch, to account for his gloominess, and Miss Bianca was temporarily reassured.

But the very next day while she was dusting in the Ambassadress's boudoir an unusual sound caught her ear: a sound as of gnawing, and by teeth more strong than any mouse's. It was a rat gnawing at the leg of the Ambassadress's favorite footstool, on which stood Omar's permanent stay-at-home cat-basket!

"Stop that at once!" ordered Miss Bianca—her famous silvery voice having for once more the ring of steel.

"Who says?" asked the rat impertinently.

"I do," said Miss Bianca—and before the fire in her eyes (shining now not like topazes, more like brown diamonds), he slunk off, but with a snarl over his shoulder that boded ill. . . .

The day after an old mouse called Roly Cheesehunter reported having seen a rat in the cellar, and another, younger mouse named Peter Pickcrumb one actually on the steps leading up to the Embassy kitchens, and on the day after that Bernard himself was ganged up on by three or four raiding the pantry. Fortunately they were only juveniles, easily dismayed by his bristling whiskers, but Algernon, who was with him, in defense of a honey pot was severely nipped on both paws.

"Of course it's possible," judged Miss Bianca, discussing these alarming events with Bernard, "that the rats intend but to make nuisances of themselves—at least I hope so! That they should

steal food and nibble footstool legs is nothing more
—but what if they *do* aim to invade the Embassy
altogether, in the Ambassador's absence? Think
what dirt and disease they'll spread, as is well
known to be their horrid practice! Is the Ambassador to return and find the Embassy little better
than a plague-pit?"

"I see what you mean," acknowledged Bernard.
"But as I said before, I don't think it's likely—a
full-scale operation, not only with Khalil on the
premises but Methuselah on guard."

"Methuselah!" exclaimed Miss Bianca contemp-
tuously. "Dear Bernard, you're as trusting as the
Ambassador! If only we knew," she added, "what
was in the rats' minds!"

There was a slight, fraught pause. Then—

"As I see you're so worried," said Bernard coolly,
"we'd better find out."

"Only how?" sighed Miss Bianca.

"Why, by infiltrating into the sewers and over-
hearing their councils," said Bernard.

Miss Bianca's whiskers trembled.

"And who is to undertake so perilous a mission?"
she asked—though already she knew the answer!

"Why, me, in rattish disguise," said bold Bernard—and at the sudden glow in her eyes felt
himself already rewarded for whatever (probably
unpleasant) the consequences of his dedicated act.

Actually Bernard didn't need much disguise. Uncommonly large for a mouse as he was—he weighed four and a half ounces—he could very well pass for a juvenile rat, except that his teeth weren't long and pointed enough. In the Scouts' dressing-up box however were a set of false ones made out of orange-peel for the use of the Demon King in their pantomimes, and these Miss Bianca carefully affixed over his own with the aid of chewing-gum. How gentle was her touch as she pressed gum to gum—and then how rewarding (in advance) her look of amazement when the operation was finished!

"My dear Bernard," cried she, "you look so like a rat I'm almost frightened of you myself! But do, do, pray take every precaution!"

Bernard would have liked to take his faithful macintosh as well—it always gave him confidence —but since no rat was known to possess such a garment he left it behind, and down into the sewers penetrated with no more protection than his own brave spirit and Miss Bianca's heartfelt prayers for his safety!

19

3

Bernard in the Sewers

IT WAS ALSO easy enough for Bernard to gain access to the sewers, by way of the cocked manhole cover and then the iron rungs below, but once down he felt almost over-awed by the majesty of his surroundings. The sewer ran towards its outlet under so nobly arching a brick roof, above granite paving-stones, it was almost like being in the nave of a cathedral! Then as he stared about him he was nearly bowled over by a press of rats all hurrying in the same direction, and sensibly letting them bear him with them, within moments arrived at what was evidently the *rats'* Moot House! It was an enclave in the riveting where the Waterboard workmen had been used to leave their

20

buckets and shovels, but was now bricked up save for a gap at ground level that afforded the rats easy entry.

At this portal stood a Tyler, or door-keeper— even for a rat very formidable looking!

"Name and number?" he challenged.

"Ninety-nine and Catchaser," said Bernard resourcefully.

"You're starting young, to call yourself Catchaser!" said the door-keeper. But he let Bernard through all the same, into a seat at the back.

If it *were* the rats' Moot House, how different from the mice's! The floor was ankle deep in dirt, even the platform at one end lacked all dignity, being nothing but an old chamber-pot turned upside down; instead of neat match-box benches were heaps of decayed potato peelings upon which the rats, instead of sitting up properly, lolled like so many tramps on park benches. However, when in Rome do as the Romans do, thought Bernard sensibly, and conquering his distaste for his surroundings he burrowed down into and then up through a heap of potato peelings and emerged looking as dirty as every one else, so no one spotted him, and at the same moment—evidently the meeting was just beginning—there strode onto the platform a very Hercules amongst rats—weighing at least eight ounces and muscled like a prize-fighter, with

on his head a helmet hammered out of a beer-bottle top, beneath which his eyes glittered like rubies. . . .

Miss Bianca's eyes glittered, or rather gleamed, like topazes, however brilliantly (except when facing an intruder) still gently. And how different her silvery tones from the harshness of the rat leader's voice as he curtly called the meeting to order!

"Rapscallions one and all," snarled he, "or should I rather call you *rat*scallions?—on your feet when I speak!"

To Bernard's surprise, the feeble jest—*rat*scallions instead of rapscallions—went down rather well. The rats not only got up but cheered, and Hercules (as Bernard was ever afterwards to think of him) surveyed them more benevolently.

"Some of you have been asking me long enough," he opened, "whether we're to do no more than spread dirt and disease through the humbler dwellings alongside the sewer. Well, I'll tell you: what we're going to do now is spread dirt and disease throughout the Embassy itself!"

"Good-oh!" cried all his hearers.

"For isn't now our opportunity," continued Hercules, "while the Ambassador and all his household staff are away? Up and about all of you—upstairs and downstairs, leave not a nook or cranny un-contaminated—and when he returns let him find a positive plague-pit!"

At this delightful prospect all the rats cheered again, while Bernard listened so horrorstruck his false teeth almost fell out.

Then up spoke a very old rat with grizzled whiskers and muzzle the color of dirty snow.

"Brilliant as is your plan, and assured of success," said he—he obviously knew the use of flattery before raising any objection—"what about the mice?"

"The mice? Phooey!" cried all the assembly.

"I trust our noble leader will hear me with more patience," said the old rat. "The mice living in the Embassy have a considerable regard for the Ambassador, who to begin with provides them with bed and board; some, one hears, are even on intimate terms with his wife and son, and may well seek to hobble so glorious a plan—"

("You bet they will!" thought Bernard.)

"—by all means in their power. Not that it amounts to much physically, we being rodent for rodent so much stronger, but they may still make nuisances of themselves." ('Twas the very phrase Miss Bianca had used about the rats!) "I therefore suggest, honored leader, that before your glorious plan is put into operation, we should deal with the mice first."

"Well thought of, old Greybeard," said Hercules. "That shall be the *first* part of our plan! And now, ere the meeting closes, for our National Anthem!"

Instantly all the rats burst into horrid song.

> *Dirt and disease!* (they yelled,)
> *Dirt and disease!*
> *Fevers and scabies,*
> *Agues and rabies,*
> *Sing ho, sing ho for the rats!*

How Bernard got himself out he never remembered, but he was sitting, as has been said, at the back, and there was no longer a warder at the door, and clutching his false teeth with both hands get out he did—first into the sewer, then up the iron rungs to the cellar, then up sweating and shaking to the Porcelain Pagoda.

"Oh Bernard," cried Miss Bianca, "how glad I am to see you safely returned! Have you gained important information?"

"Indeed I have," panted Bernard, at last thankfully casting aside all disguise (i.e., his false teeth). "The rats *do* mean to invade the Embassy!"

"And what shall we do to foil them?" cried Miss

25

Bianca with flashing eye—for it never occurred to her to take so dreadful a prospect lying down, even if the Radish Patch indeed awaited!

"In the first place," replied Bernard, "call a Special General Meeting of the M.P.A.S.!"

It was called for the very next midnight, midnight always being the time when mice are most active and alert.—How did the rats get wind of it? Had they too infiltrated a spy? But the explanation, as will be seen, was far simpler. . . .

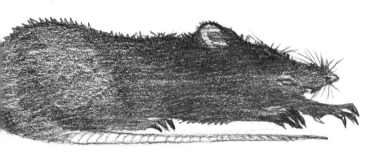

4

The Special General Meeting

ALL NEXT DAY the M.P.A.S. Scouts hurried
hither and thither posting summonses through
letter-boxes, and not one was unheeded.—One
specially wasn't unheeded, the one a Scout acci-
dentally dropped down a rubbish-chute, and which
was found by a rat on the rubbish-tip! But all the
others reached their proper destinations, and never
had the Moot House been fuller than when Bernard rose to address his assembled troops—for so
he thought of them already, though they themselves didn't yet know that that was what they
were going to be expected to be. The Moot House
was so full because of a rumor that Miss Bianca

would be present, and mothers even brought their children to hear her famous silvery voice. " 'Twill be something to remember all your lives," promised the mothers, "that you heard the famous Miss Bianca speak!" So the Moot House was so full, the spigot in the claret cask's bunghole had to be left pulled out to admit air.

And there Miss Bianca was indeed, seated on the platform with the other members of the Committee, for though she now rarely attended General Meetings the gravity of the occasion impelled her to be present at this one, and all the mice were so pleased to see her the proceedings opened with a burst of clapping obviously directed to her personally. Miss Bianca of course rose and bowed, but immediately turned to Bernard with a gesture indicating that he, not she, was the one to be listened to.

"Fellow members of the M.P.A.S.," opened Bernard, "though I know you're all glad to see Miss Bianca once again amongst us—"

"Indeed we are!" cried all the members of the Ladies' Guild. "Hooray for Miss Bianca!" shouted the Scouts, headed by a young half-Irish mouse named Shaun; for they'd never forgotten how she'd once restored their pride in themselves by making them agents in the rehabilitation of the wicked steward Mandrake, now honestly employed in rolling an Orphanage tennis-court.*

"—you'd better shut up and give me your full attention," proceeded Bernard. "There's only one item on our agenda: and it's rats."

To the clapping and cheering now succeeded an uneasy silence. All mice fear and detest rats, as all respectable citizens fear and detest outlaws of any kind. Mice live in neat holes—villa-residences, as it were—whereas rats sleep out rough, and their well-known spreading of dirt and disease was a natural consequence. At Bernard's word a wave of apprehension swept through the entire assembly.

"There is no need for panic," continued Bernard, "but the fact remains that more than one rat has already been seen on the Embassy premises. How they gain entry we know: by way of the cellar, as our esteemed member Roly Cheesehunter can bear witness."

Old Roly Cheesehunter, pushed to his feet by a daughter-in-law, rose and bobbed his head.

"In the cellar 'twas indeed I saw one," affirmed he, "combing of his whiskers bold as brass!"

"Peter Pickcrumb I think can bear witness too?" prompted Bernard.

* See *The Turret.*

29

"The one *I* saw was halfway up the cellar steps!" corroborated young Pickcrumb. "Not that he stayed long, for didn't I soon bowl him over!"

He omitted to add that the rat in question had been looking the other way when suddenly barged into from behind. Actually both had been taken by surprise, as the rat tumbled off and Peter Pickcrumb gaped down after him!

"Not to panic," repeated Bernard, "but I happen to know"— he was too modest to explain *how* he knew—"that the rats intend, in the Ambassador's absence, to take over the Embassy altogether, spreading as usual dirt and disease until it becomes little better than a plague-pit. Is this to be allowed?"

"No, no!" cried all the mice, quite carried away by his eloquence.

"I therefore propose," went on Bernard, "that besides putting a guard in the cellar we at once form posses of vigilantes who will be at all times armed—"

"What with?" asked a voice from the back.

"Arms will be provided," said Bernard. "The posses will be on duty, naturally turn and turn about, twenty-four hours a day, any fresh glimpse or sign of a rat to be immediately reported to me at Headquarters in my flat. These are merely precautions," he added, "but better make sure than be sorry. And now will all ready to do vigilante-duty sign their names on the forms provided."

There was an absolute rush to sign. Fathers of families, gay young bachelors, even ancients like Roly Cheesehunter and of course every one of the Scouts, had to be marshalled into a queue. "What about us?" cried all the members of the Ladies' Guild. "Are we to play no part?" "Your part will be to tend the wounded," said Bernard, "that is, if there are any. You might start by getting a few bandages ready. . . ."

All were so busy and excited, no one had an ear for anything going on outside; but in a brief silence after the last of the forms was completed Bernard suddenly cocked his whiskers.

"Does anyone else hear anything?" he asked.

Now all listened, and from without indeed heard a pattering of feet—or not exactly a pattering, rather a trampling, rhythmic tread. Then they heard several gruff orders given in a voice of authority—the voice, Bernard recognized, of Hercules!

"Shin up to the Look-out, Shaun," said Bernard, he hoped casually, "and see what's going on."

The Look-out was a crack high up where two of the claret cask's staves had warped apart. Willingly Shaun shinned up to it—but shinned down with his fur staring. . . .

"It's the rats!" gasped he. "Scores and scores of them, and marching in order, as if they meant to launch an attack!"

So swiftly had the rats, alerted by that one summons gone astray, put their plan into action— striking where the mice felt themselves most secure and hoping to wipe them out at one fell swoop!

Immediately, inside the Moot House, all was confusion and dismay, as mothers agitatedly clasped their little ones to their bosoms and even those newly enlisted as vigilantes trembled. But Bernard kept his head.

"The spigot!" he ordered. "All hands to re-place the spigot in the bunghole!"

All hands—or at least sufficient—obeyed, and within seconds the spigot was shoved back. 'Twas of oak, a wood hard enough to blunt even rats' teeth, as the latter soon found out, for nibble and chew as they might—launching the attack indeed! —the heart of oak defeated them, so the Moot House was impregnable!

Within, all the mice began to draw breath again, and Miss Bianca to compose a poem in praise of acorns.

BEGINNING OF A POEM WRITTEN BY
MISS BIANCA IN PRAISE OF ACORNS

O tiny seeds of mighty trees
  Whose pith withstands e'en rattish teeth
    How wond'rous Nature's feat!
  Behold the oak!—and see beneath
Its spreading branches cattle too at ease
    Shelt'ring from noonday heat!
Whilst its roots small flowerlets twinkle,
The primrose, violet and periwinkle!

It will be seen that Miss Bianca had embarked
on a rather ambitious rhyme-scheme, and as she
began the second stanza—

O tiny seeds whose ridgèd cups
  Hold dormant power unequaled—

she knew she was going to run into difficulties.
But before she had begun to tackle them both she
and all the other mice became aware that something else was going on outside again.

Or rather, *not* going on . . .

To sounds of (frustrated) nibbling and gnawing had now succeeded complete silence.

A somehow ominous silence.

Yet there had been no sound of the rats making
off.

"Shin up again, Shaun," said Bernard.

So up once more shinned Shaun, and once more shinned down with ill news.

"They've all settled down on their hunkers," reported he, "but still in ranks. I'd say—a frontal attack having failed—they mean to encamp where they are and starve us out!"

Such indeed was the rats' new strategy, and as the mice realized it again they trembled. They were safe enough for the moment, only however were they to get out? But Bernard had an idea.

"*Remove* the spigot," ordered he. "Remove the spigot—"

"What, our only defense?"cried the mice.

"—and bring forth the Gorgonzola!"

Again he was obeyed—and truly proud of him felt Miss Bianca (even though interrupted in the middle of composing a poem) as he so masterfully took command. From underneath the platform obedient hands hauled forth the by this time riper-than-ripe cheese, whilst others tugged at the spigot, which came out with a pop like a cork coming out of a bottle, and for heart of oak was substituted heart of Gorgonzola!

'Twas indeed a gallant cheese. Its fumes proved so deadly, the rats succumbed as before a gas-attack. Those in front fell sideways from their hunkers with all four feet in the air, and even the

35

rearmost ranks choked and spluttered but a moment before following suit, and within a moment more all were *hors de combat* (which is French for being down and out). Even Hercules was *hors de combat,* he the foremost of all having received the Gorgonzola's full blast absolutely *nez à nez* (which is French for head on), and lay senseless upon what should have been his field of victory!

"Now is our chance!" cried Bernard, seizing Miss Bianca by the wrist. "Women and children first, but all evacuate!"

Upon which mouse after mouse, holding their whiskers over their noses, tiptoed out over and between the prostrate bodies of their foes and then made a dash for the cellar steps and safety above.—Bernard would have been the last to leave, if he hadn't had Miss Bianca to look after. As it was, he and she were the last but one to leave, being followed only by old Roly Cheesehunter who was so rheumatical he could scarcely hobble.

5

Warlike Preparations

THUS THE FIRST open confrontation between the rats and the mice ended in victory for the mice, in that the Moot House had been neither taken by force nor reduced to surrender. All the same it was not so much in triumph as in dismay that Bernard and Miss Bianca consulted together next morning in the Porcelain Pagoda.

"For will not the rats return to the attack?" asked she nervously.

"If I know anything of Hercules," said Bernard, "that's for sure. But right away he's got to get his troops on their feet again and back into the sewers where they can feel safe and renew their ardor. What *we* must do, even before we arm ourselves,

39

is set a sentry in the cellar. Only who's to take on so responsible a post? Roly Cheesehunter, for all his sterling qualities, is too old, and Shaun too harum-scarum. I'd do it myself, but that I'm going to have my hands full issuing weapons and organizing the posses."

"*I*," said Miss Bianca, "had thought of Khalil. . . ."

Bernard stared.

"What, a snake off a snakes-and-ladders board?" he exclaimed. "A mere gamester?"

"Did not Algernon tell how but the sight of his nose frightened at least one rat away?" argued Miss Bianca. "Stationed at the man-hole over the main drain, mightn't he frighten off whole hordes of them?"

"I believe you've got something," said Bernard. "The point is, will Khalil cooperate? Still, it's worth trying, and I'll go and tackle him at the Club at once."

Small persuasion however needed Khalil when the proposition was put to him, for he often found the inside of the Boy's play-box too noisy for reptilian comfort. Down into the cellar he followed Bernard—rippling down the steps like a rill of water where Bernard had to cling and jump—and hissed his appreciation of the quiet.

There wasn't a rat in sight—evidently Hercules *had* got them all back into the sewers!—but as Bernard introduced Khalil to his post, he was too conscientious not to warn the snake that one or two might appear.

"Pssha! What if they do?" returned Khalil. "My grandpappy used to eat a dozen rats just as a snack between breakfast and lunch!"

It struck Bernard that Khalil's granddad must have been several sizes larger than Khalil, but he refrained from saying so, trusting, like Miss Bianca, that the mere sight of a reptile would frighten the rats away, and Khalil coiled himself over the man-hole looking if anything rather greedy!

Then Bernard went to take a look at the Moot House—and found that the rats had recovered

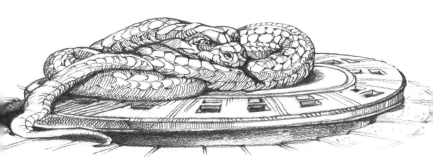

their ardor even sooner than could have been expected. . . .

For only some twelve hours had elapsed since the great claret cask stood proud and impregnable, and now what a shambles met his infuriated gaze! The rats must have squeezed, to get through the left-open bunghole, but once inside they had wrought absolute havoc—smashing the match-box benches into smithereens and turning the armchairs on the platform upside down, and worst of all defacing the Moot House's chief treasure, the oil painting of a lion being freed from a net by a mouse, by scrawling it over with rude words, also the slogan "Up the Rats!"

"They shall pay for this," thought Bernard grimly.

However, he didn't feel like sending in a cleaning-up party quite immediately. The man-hole cover was still a-cock, and unlike Miss Bianca he wasn't entirely convinced that Khalil's mere presence would suffice to frighten the rats off. So he said nothing to her about the desecration of the premises she'd so recently graced, but devoted all his energies to arming and organizing his own troops.

For weapons he drew chiefly on a box of pennibs newly opened on the ambassador's desk. Bernard, living as has been said in the Ambassador's

old cigar cabinet, naturally knew his way about
the Ambassador's desk as well as he'd once known
his way about the Embassy pantries, and since it
was in the Ambassador's own interest he was act-
ing, had no hesitation in making free with his pen-
nibs. Some, lashed to match-sticks, formed pikes,
others (if the match-stick broke off short, as it
often did), daggers, and within twenty-four hours
all mice who'd signed forms were armed to the
teeth and under Bernard's leadership began to
drill.

All the mice entrusted with pikes thoroughly
enjoyed drilling, though even to begin with the
orders Stand Ready, Advance Pikes and Charge
often brought the rear rank into painful collision
with the front (painful to the front rank, that is),
while those who had only daggers, such as the
Scouts, borrowed their mothers' go-to-market
cloaks and formed cloak-and-dagger units. The
mice were indeed embattled against the rats, and
many anticipated the coming confrontation quite
with glee!

That is, the younger and more foolhardy
amongst them. Their seniors knew better what foes
they faced. . . .

"And am I to take no part in these martial ac-
tivities?" asked Algernon discontentedly.

43

"My dear old chap," said Bernard, "no one less than I doubts your courage and resource, both so brilliantly displayed in the Wolf Range. But in action against rats, what above all is needed is agility."

Algernon looked glum, for he certainly wasn't very agile. He was too stout.

"I think I should at least be pwovided with a weapon," said he—lapsing for once into the lisp he'd got rid of in the Wolf Range.

"And a weapon you shall have," Bernard assured him. "One made specially!"

The special weapon made for Algernon was a pen-nib lashed not to a match-stick but to a pencil, and he drilled with it till he could present arms as smartly as a Guardsman outside Buckingham Palace in his native London—which would be a fat lot of use, thought Bernard, if ever there *were* an invasion by rats! Nonetheless, with all his troops armed to the teeth, and with Khalil on watch, Bernard began to feel much more comfortable, and only on one point still anxious.

"There's something I must absolutely insist on," said he to Miss Bianca. "Henceforward, until the war is over, you mustn't stir a step from the Porcelain Pagoda!"

"What, when such heroic action is afoot?" exclaimed Miss Bianca indignantly. "Of course I must be among you—if not in actual hand-to-hand combat, at least to encourage and inspire! Think of Joan of Arc!"

"I'm sorry," said Bernard, "but it's out of the question. If *you* were captured by rats, I for one would feel no price, even total surrender, too high to pay to ransom you, so we mustn't risk it. Joan of Arc," he added, "as far as I remember, *wasn't* ransomed, and came to a sad end on a bonfire. I couldn't bear to think of *you* on a bonfire, Miss Bianca! So just stay here as safe as possible and water your garden. Will you promise me?"

Seeing him so concerned, and wishing above all things to free his mind for the important duties that now engaged it, of course Miss Bianca promised; but as soon as he was gone composed a brief poem that embodied all her own distress.

BRIEF POEM COMPOSED BY MISS BIANCA
IN DISTRESS OF MIND

*The Embassy our kindly home attacked by rattish
        foes*
Shall I with watering-can stand idly by?
No, no! 'Twere shame! Rather let ev'ry rose
Pansy and violet wither, droop and die!

45

As Miss Bianca was very fond of her garden, it will be seen how strongly she felt; how *could* she stand idly by? But she had given Bernard her word, and was too much of a lady (or gentleman) to break it. Was there nothing she could do *without* leaving the Porcelain Pagoda?

Miss Bianca was always realistic. She fully appreciated the bravery of the mice, and how wise and resourceful would be Bernard's leadership, but rodent for rodent the rats were so much stronger, and there were so many of them!

"Undoubtedly we shall need allies," thought Miss Bianca, "and whose fault is it after all that the Embassy is put in such dire peril?"

So she wrote a letter to the Waterworks Board.

Miss Bianca's handwriting was so small, it was doubtful whether any Waterworks Board employee would be able to decipher it, but Nigel (whose moustache, under the application of Pomade Divine, had already sprouted a slight fuzz), wrote a fair round hand enough, and him Miss Bianca enlisted to take dictation on note-paper abstracted from the Ambassador's desk with envelope to match.

Dear Sirs: (dictated Miss Bianca)
    Unless your underlings immediately re-

46

place in its proper position the man-hole cover
in the cellar of this Embassy, the case will be
taken up by the United Nations.

"That ought to produce results!" said Nigel
admiringly. "How do we sign?"

"Simply with the Ambassador's official stamp,"
said Miss Bianca, "that he signs everything with!"

The impression was a bit faint, owing to the
inking-pad's having a little dried up, but nonetheless perfectly legible, and no postage stamp was
needed since a Scout delivered it by hand at the
Waterworks offices next day.—Unfortunately it
was the same Scout who'd dropped a summons
down a rubbish-chute, and he now pushed it
through the slot marked Circulars Only. . . .

It will be seen that Miss Bianca's anxieties were
all on her friends' behalf; little did she think that
she herself might be in immediate, deadly peril!

6

Miss Bianca in Peril!

FOR BERNARD'S FEARS for her were not un-
founded. Of course all the rats knew about Miss
Bianca's special position as patroness of the
M.P.A.S., and the thought of capturing her and
holding her for ransom had more than once
crossed Hercules's mind; he'd actually organized a
special squad of kidnappers ready to seize any
chance that offered, but hitherto, faithful to her
word, she'd never set foot outside the Porcelain
Pagoda, so they never had one, but could only
lurk outside the Embassy in hopes.

Now, however, what with anxiety and lack of
fresh air, Miss Bianca had begun to grow paler

and paler—not actually paler, she being snow white already; say rather that her ermine coat began to lose its gloss—and Bernard in alarm consented to her walking out for twenty minutes or so each day in the Radish Patch, which permission he gave the more readily because the Radish Patch was surrounded by practically a *cheval-de-frise* of close-set holly bushes beyond which she promised never to venture. All the same, he usually accompanied her himself, or put Shaun on duty as bodyguard; but one morning, bored with waiting for one or the other to fetch her, in a spirit of independence Miss Bianca went out into the Radish Patch alone—little suspecting that on the other side of the holly hedge half a dozen fierce rats lurked waiting for a chance to kidnap her!

'Twas a sad enough spot to take an airing in—dotted with little mounds beneath which fledglings and bumblebees lay buried, surrounding the bigger ones that commemorated a hedgehog and a tortoise, and Miss Bianca's mind, always well stocked with poetry, turned gratefully to Gray's "Elegy Written in a Country Churchyard."

"The boast of heraldry, the pomp of pow'r," Miss Bianca repeated to herself,

And all that beauty, all that wealth e'er gave,

Awaits alike th' inevitable hour:
  The paths of glory lead but to the grave.

"How true!" thought Miss Bianca. "Still"—and here she thought of Bernard and his heroic determination to face the rattish foe—"better to have followed a path of glory *first!*"

Then she went on to her favorite bit, about far from the madding crowd's ignoble strife, but even here put in a rider.

"For not all strife is ignoble," thought Miss Bianca. "Some, in defense of one's hearth and home, for instance, is actually praiseworthy!"

At which point her meditations were interrupted by a rat's creeping in between the roots of the holly bushes. . . .

He was so very small a rat (otherwise he wouldn't have been able to penetrate them), Miss Bianca took him for a mouse, and a mouse-pedlar at that, for round his neck he had slung a tray of trinkets; and being always compassionate of such poor wayfarers, Miss Bianca for a moment regarded his geegaws with a kindly eye. But what were mere strings of beads to one who wore the Ambassadress's silver chain about her neck? So, though still kindly, she set them aside. . . .

51

"Come with me," persuaded the pretended ped-lar, "and I'll show you better!"

But Miss Bianca only shook her head, and after a moment he made off, and Miss Bianca returned to her poetic meditations.

"For who, to dumb forgetfulness a prey," repeated Miss Bianca to herself,

This pleasing anxious being e'er resigned,
Left the warm precincts of the cheerful day,
Nor cast one longing ling'ring look behind?

"Well, I don't imagine any of the fledglings did," thought Miss Bianca, more cheerfully. "The poor little things can hardly have seen daylight at all!— and as for the hedgehog, perhaps *his* anxieties— continually dodging traffic!—were less pleasing than painful!"

At which point in her now more cheerful medi-tations there crept out from between the holly roots another very small rat, whom again Miss Bianca took for a mouse, this time in widow's weeds.

"Kind lady," she pleaded, "may I just see, won't you show me, where my dear late husband is buried?"

At such an appeal, how could Miss Bianca's tender heart not melt? It was with genuine regret that she replied that unless the late lamented had

53

been either a fledgling or a hedgehog or a tortoise (on the face of it improbable), she was afraid she couldn't.

"Then it must be somewhere else," wept the pretended widow, "though I was distinctly told the Radish Patch, in the Embassy grounds—and what an honor, I thought, for my poor old man! But perhaps it's just outside he lies, in the rough ground *beyond* this horrid hedge! Kind lady, won't you come and help me look?—for I'm so blind with crying I can hardly see an inch before my nose!"

Miss Bianca felt so sorry for her, she was indeed advancing to the roots of the holly hedge— beyond which a party of rats waited to kidnap her! —when her silver chain caught on a holly prickle, and as she paused to disentangle it she remembered how she'd given her word to Bernard not to stir a foot beyond the Radish Patch. . . .

"You must forgive me," said Miss Bianca, "if I leave you to make your sad pilgrimage alone, followed only by my every good wish!"

So it was perhaps the Ambassadress's gift that saved Miss Bianca from being kidnapped!

She said nothing to Bernard, when he came hurrying to join her, of either incident, but on thinking them over began to wonder whether either pedlar or widow were what they pretended to be, which suspicions made her so uneasy she voluntarily declared that she was feeling so much better for her airings, she wouldn't need to walk in the Radish Patch again—which was a great relief to Bernard's mind.

Yet so tender was her heart, the subsequent fate of both pretended pedlar and pretended widow would have distressed her extremely, had she known of it, for Hercules was so angered by their failure to lure her from safety, he ordered both their tails to be cut off!

Well it was that Bernard's mind was relieved on one point, for he almost immediately had a new crisis to cope with. . . .

7

Broken Reeds

THE NEXT DAY in fact passed rather peacefully: with Khalil on guard, Bernard felt able to give his troops a stand-easy, to allow them a brief period of normal domestic life; the Ladies' Guild paused in making bandages to begin making jam, and the Scouts began to discuss their coming pantomime. For twenty-four hours, it was quite like old times!

But for twenty-four hours only. At dawn next morning the valiant Hercules—for however wicked he was undeniably valiant—himself led a party of the largest and fiercest rats in a desperate onslaught on the snake's soft under-belly,

biting and worrying and worrying and biting until
Khalil didn't know whether he was on his head
or his tail, and at last was only thankful to slither
up the cellar steps (like a rill of water in reverse),
and then up till he regained the safety of the Boy's
play-box, where, to the indignation of Algernon,
he coiled his whole twelve inches underneath the
snakes-and-ladders board. . . .

"Deserter!" cried Algernon. "Faithless to your
post! Sentries have been shot for less!"

"We snakes have a reputation for faithlessness,"
pointed out Khalil smoothly, "and I thought for
once it might as well be deserved. If *you* had four
or five fierce rats attacking your tum, I dare say
you'd be no braver than I was!"

In this he was wrong, as will be seen, but for
the moment Algernon was in too much of a hurry
to relay the news to tick the reptile off as he
deserved.

"Khalil has deserted his post," he told Bernard,
whom he found delivering cream cheese to Miss
Bianca in her Porcelain Pagoda. "The man-hole
is unguarded, and the rats may attack whenever
they choose!"

"Oh, faithless, faithless Khalil!" cried Miss
Bianca. "Now we are indeed in peril!"

But Bernard, who had never entirely trusted

the snake, kept his cool, and after hurrying off to make a fresh review of his forces, returned looking almost cheerful.

"Roly Cheesehunter," reported Bernard, "and I must say he's a bit of an old hero, has volunteered to stand by with the bicycle bell."

It was actually a tricycle bell, off the Boy's old tricycle the Boy had discarded when he graduated to two wheels, and which like many other bits and pieces had become the property of the mice; and Roly Cheesehunter was confident that by striking it with a pen-nib dagger he would be able to arouse the whole Embassy in time. . . .

"In time for what?" asked Miss Bianca.

"Why, for us mice to assemble and *repulse* the rats!" said Bernard. "But one thing again I must ask you to promise me: if you hear any kind of rumpus going on, you won't try to join in—never mind about Joan of Arc!—but just stay safe in bed."

Seeing him so urgent—his whiskers suddenly quivering—how could Miss Bianca refuse? So she promised.

"And that repulse them we undoubtedly shall," added Bernard encouragingly, "I haven't the slightest doubt!"

"Nor I," agreed Algernon stoutly. "We'll make mincemeat of them!"

Miss Bianca wished she could share their optimism, but still felt allies would be needed, and nothing yet had been heard from the Waterworks Board. . . .

But perhaps another ally was at hand, for who should come strolling in that same evening but Omar!

Cat though he was, and mouse as she was, Miss Bianca was no more nervous of him than she'd been of her old friend Shah—sporting with whom she'd been used to make, everyone said, the prettiest picture in the world!—but they were not yet on intimate terms, and she greeted him at first with less warmth than surprise.

"Why aren't you in the country with the Ambassadress?" she asked.

"My dear, the country's such a bore you can't imagine!" yawned Omar, showing pearly teeth set in rose-petal colored gums. (He was undoubtedly a beautiful cat indeed, as well he knew!) "Nothing to see, nothing to do, birds waking one up at all hours! I simple couldn't stand it any longer, so I came back."

It is well known that cats can find their way home across even miles and miles of unfamiliar territory, so there was nothing special about Omar's achievement (though he looked as pleased with himself as though there were), and Miss Bianca wasn't impressed. But as a sudden idea occurred to her, she flattered him by pretending to be quite amazed.

"All that way on foot!" she marvelled.

"Well, not actually on *foot*," admitted Omar. "I got a lift in a rather nice sports car, whose driver, when he read the tag on my collar, seemed quite pleased to drop me at the Embassy—though a little disappointed, I fear, to find no one but Methuselah at home!"

"And you come absolutely at the right time," cried Miss Bianca impetuously, "to help defend the Embassy against the rats!"

Omar blinked his beautiful eyes.

"The Embassy troubled by rats?" said he disapprovingly. "Why ever did you let them in?"

"We didn't *let* them in," said Miss Bianca. "However, 'tis too long a tale to tell, and now *you* are returned all may yet be well! I should have thought of a cat sooner!"

Omar however was lending but half an ear (he never lent more to anything that promised disagreeableness), and with a wave of his plumy tail went off to the Ambassador's bathroom and jumped up on the wash-basin and put his paw inside the medicine-chest to get at the Ambassador's Pomade Divine, for it was the only thing he trusted to pre-

61

serve his beautiful white fluffy coat, and the Ambassador had forgotten to pack it. Omar was such a dandy he'd probably have come back on that account alone, even without the nuisance of birdsong!—and in his eagerness made such a clatter among the other jars and bottles, Algernon came to see what was going on.

"What, *you* back?" said Algernon. "I thought you were still in the country?"

Omar was just going into his piece about country dullness when he noticed the fresh scars on Algernon's paws.

"You seem to have been a bit in the wars," remarked he. "Try some iodine."

"Of course I've been in the wars," retorted Algernon. "There's a war *on*."

"Miss Bianca told me something of the sort," said Omar, beginning to rub the Pomade Divine deep into his coat. "Something about trouble with rats . . . You don't mean to tell me those are *rat-bites?*"

"Oh, just a few nips," said Algernon carelessly. "If you want to see what they can really do, take a look at Khalil's tum!"

"There is nothing I should like less," said Omar distastefully, "than to look at Khalil's tum."

"Still I'm sure Miss Bianca's glad to see you back," said Algernon, "as indeed I am myself.

Why ever," he echoed her, "didn't we think of a cat sooner?"

Upon which the bear went off to rejoice with Nigel over their new-found ally, and Omar, as soon as his coat was thoroughly shampooed, left the bathroom to seek repose in his own special basket in the Ambassadress's boudoir.

Where he noticed one leg of the footstool on which it stood definitely wobbling, and as Bernard came in on his now nightly round of inspection, enquired rather censoriously whether the Embassy furniture had become a prey to wood-worm.

"Not wood-worm, rats," corrected Bernard. "My word, what teeth they have! I'm glad to see you back," he added. "At least the Ambassadress's boudoir is safe to-night!"

Then he went off again, leaving Omar feeling more than a little uneasy. At first, he was so conceited, he had thought it only natural everyone should be so pleased to see him back, but he now began to realize that he too was expected to engage in warfare against the rats!—and the idea didn't appeal to him in the least. Were *his* velvet paws to be scarred like Algernon's, was *his* beautiful furry tum to suffer the fate of Khalil's? Omar shuddered at the thought, and wished with all his heart he'd never returned to the Embassy at all!

All through the night, every time he turned round in his basket it so wobbled he couldn't get forty winks; and at dawn next morning, even on foot, started on his way back to the country—dullness and bird-song and all!

He was undeservedly lucky in that now a Post Office van gave him a lift. "Though mind you keep your claws off the mail," adjured the Postman, "or I'll set you down in the middle of nowhere!" But he recognized Omar as a member of the Ambassadorial household whither he was bound with a sackful of diplomatic correspondence, and his bark was worse than his bite, and so Omar returned to the pettings of the Ambassadress, who'd been quite concerned by his overnight absence, leaving the beleaguered Embassy just as beleaguered as before.

"It was only to be expected," said Bernard, when he and Miss Bianca discovered next morning that Omar had vamoosed. "I thought he looked a bit unhappy when I explained to him about the footstool. Cats always think of themselves first."

"I'm sure *Shah* wouldn't have," cried Miss Bianca, warm in defense of her late lamented friend. "If only Shah were here, never, never would he have deserted us!"

"Only he isn't here," said Bernard. "And more

to the point, neither is Omar. We mice are on our own—and a good thing too!"

Much as she admired his confidence, Miss Bianca still couldn't help feeling that some reinforcements wouldn't come amiss; and thinking and thinking—still no sign from the Waterworks Board—now thought not of cats but of dogs.

"Terriers!" thought Miss Bianca. "Are not terriers quite famous foes of rats?"

Unfortunately she didn't know any terriers. She didn't know any dogs at all: the Ambassador's old pointer was always kept in the country, and Miss Bianca had never so much as set eyes on him.

But wasn't there a Dog Show taking place at that very moment—the same Dog Show the Boy had so regretted missing?

8

Shaun at the Dog Show

"SHAUN," PROPOSED MISS Bianca that afternoon (though without mentioning her scheme to Bernard), "you who know your way about the city so well, could you not infiltrate yourself into the Dog Show?"

"At the Agricultural Hall? Easy as kiss your hand!" said Shaun.

"And then perhaps suggest to any terriers there —for there is sure to be a class for terriers!—that after the proceedings are over, they'd find some excellent ratting here at the Embassy?"

"Not a one would refuse the chance!" declared Shaun. "If I know anything of terriers, they'd not *wait* for the proceedings to be over!"

"Then go and do your best," said Miss Bianca. "Conduct them to the back door, which Methuselah alas always leaves ajar, and then down to the cellar by the shortest route. Of course no rats may immediately appear—"

"Terriers'll scent them all right," promised Shaun, "even through a foot of concrete! And if we all together managed to shove the man-hole cover a bit more aside, why shouldn't they jump down and slay the rats in the very sewers where they belong?"

Miss Bianca felt so encouraged by this conversation, she did something she hadn't done for days—put her feet up in a hammock under a parasol in the Porcelain Pagoda's pleasure ground!

Shaun got into the Dog Show as easily as Bernard had got into the sewers; for when he reached the big entrance gate of the Agricultural Hall the proceedings were almost over, and even the Commissionaire on duty had gone inside to watch the final judging—all eyes were indeed so fixed on the show ring, no one would have noticed a tiger coming in, let alone a mouse! (Unlike Bernard, Shaun made no attempt at disguise; he was too small to try to look like even a Chinese sleeve-dog.) Another piece of luck for him was that the two potential champions were a Wolfhound and a

Saluki, so all smaller dogs were back on their benches, where even their owners had abandoned them to watch who would be the winner! Thus Shaun was able to approach unobserved the terrier-class section, where he at once overheard two of Scottish breed exchanging disobliging remarks about Ivor (the Wolfhound) and Riza Khan (the Saluki).

"A gey lot of use wad either of *them* be," said Rory, "in a hill mist on the fells, wi' hair o'er their een like a leddy's veil!"

"Pit one o' *their* lang legs down a coneyhole," agreed Hamish, "and 'twould snap like a chicken-bone!"

"Too high off the ground altogether!" criticized Rory.

"Too *fancy* altogether!" criticized Hamish.

"I couldna' agree wi' ye more," said Shaun, adopting for the moment a Scottish accent to match.

Both Hamish and Rory looked round—first up, then down, but to Shaun's relief only with surprise, not annoyance, at his butting in.

"Wee, sleekit, cow'rin' tim'rous beastie!" exclaimed Hamish. "Thou need na start awa sae hasty!"

Shaun, who didn't know Hamish was quoting the famous poet Robert Burns, was rather offended; he didn't at all like being called either timorous or cowering, and he hadn't started away, but was standing pat.

"Actually I'm here to bring you an invitation," said he, "to join a ratting party—"

The ears of both terriers pricked!

"—in a cellar not far off. It occurred to me that after your long boring day a little relaxation might be welcome?"

"Ye can say that again!" exclaimed Hamish.

"After being paraded up and doon before that eediot of a judge!" chimed in Rory.

"Then follow me!" instructed Shaun.

No second bidding needed either. They weren't now leashed to their benches—their owners had been too excited by the final judging to see to it— and down both jumped and streaked out from the Dog Show in Shaun's wake just as the judge declared an equal tie and the assembly broke up!

"Oh, where is my Rory?" cried Rory's owner.

"Oh, where is my Hamish?" cried Hamish's.

Upon which both owners, glimpsing Rory's and Hamish's rapidly vanishing tails, pelted in pursuit, and if it had been only Rory's owner in pursuit the ratting party might well have got away, for she was too old and stout to run fast; but Hamish's owner was a lean young hockey-playing type, and got her foot on his lead just as he reached

the exit, pulling him up with such a jerk he was nearly strangled, at the same time reaching out a long skinny arm to seize Rory by the scruff, and they were both borne back into bondage!

What the hockey-player would have done to Shaun, had she noticed him, and particularly if she'd realized his part in the escapade, is best left to the imagination!

Thus Shaun had to return to the Porcelain Pagoda and report mission failed.

"Though both were ready and willing," lamented he. "Keen as mustard the pair of them! 'Twas only that skinny giraffe of a female that hobbled us!"

"Good Shaun, I know you did your best," said Miss Bianca kindly—but also sadly, for she had counted more than she liked to admit on canine allies. Omar, and the Waterworks Board, and now the Dog Show, all had proved broken reeds, and where was she to turn next? Yet Bernard still seemed so confident, Miss Bianca could only express her private apprehensions in a poem she composed in bed that night when she couldn't sleep.

Brave Bernard and embattled mice,
Prepared to do or die,

None doubts your valor less than I!
But when I think that rats are twice
Your size at least, or even thrice,
A tear starts to my eye!

She had barely completed it when, just at midnight, up from the cellar the alarm-bell sounded!

9
The Battle of the Cellar Steps

HOW THANKFUL WAS Bernard that none of the mice proved broken reeds, but absolutely fell over themselves to get down to the cellar to repulse the rattish foe! Himself of course led the van, but the posses of vigilantes weren't far behind, nor Shaun and the Scouts—all ready, in Miss Bianca's words, to do or die!

"Pikes and daggers at the ready, charge!" yelled Bernard.

The mice charged, and the first wave of rats issuing from the sewers indeed wavered—but only momentarily. Though they had no such sophisticated weapons they didn't need them, rodent for rodent (also in Miss Bianca's words) being so much the heavier.—She herself at the sound of the alarm bell immediately jumped out of bed and threw on a swansdown negligee; then remembering her promise to Bernard threw it off and got back between her pink silk sheets, where all she could do was pray for a mouse victory!

Alas, her prayers were needed. Many a pen-nib indeed found its mark in rattish vitals, but even a rat struck to the heart could ere he succumbed still bowl his assailant over and leave it to a fellow-rat to administer the bite, or *coup de grâce.* In the very firsh clash old Roly Cheesehunter, still heroically banging on the tricycle bell, was laid low, then Peter Pickcrumb, while Shaun, tackling Hercules himself, was trampled down almost without Hercules' noticing him. . . .

"Pikes and daggers at the ready, charge again!" yelled Bernard desperately.

But by now a second wave of rats was advancing, and even Bernard's well-drilled troops were forced to retreat back and back towards the cellar steps, though still fighting every inch of the way. Among individual deeds of heroism almost too numerous to detail, one was outstanding: a vigilante with his pike broken short rammed the butt down his assailant's throat and ere he succumbed himself had choked a rat to death! A word also must be said of the Scouts, who back to back in close formation presented their daggers like the prickles of a hedgehog and offered a serious obstacle in the path of the enemy. But they too were overwhelmed by superior weight and forced to give ground, though still in close order, up and up the cellar steps. . . .

At the head of which stood Algernon presenting arms!

He did more than present them. With his bayonet made from a pen-nib lashed to a pencil he lunged left and right, quite disregarding any rat-bites on his tum (so sucks to Khalil!).

"Have at ye, ye filthy vermin!" shouted Algernon. "Back to the sewers where ye belong!"

And back indeed the rats retreated—but again only momentarily, for now advanced Hercules at the head of his *corps d'élite* (again French, meaning his best troops) and in a head-on collision knocked Algernon for six. But though knocked down the gallant bear wasn't knocked out, and even before Bernard could rush to his aid was on his legs again yelling, "Up the Mice!"

"Up the Mice!" shouted Bernard too, as now absolutely on the cellar steps the battle raged and swayed with redoubled fury. The Battle of Waterloo was nothing to it—and as at Waterloo, the issue hung in the balance unless reinforcements arrived—as they suddenly did, though 'twas not

75

Blücher's troops that turned the tide, but the arrival of a Waterworks employee!

At last Miss Bianca's letter had reached its destination. An intelligent Water Board secretary, sorting out the offers of free breakfast food in the Circulars Only box, recognized the Ambassadorial envelope and placed it in the in-tray of her superior, who in turn, alarmed by the reference to the United Nations, instructed a Waterworks underling to take immediate action. It wasn't quite immediate action the Waterworks underling took, because all that day there were several leaks in the main drain as well he had to see to, after which he had a date to take his girl-friend out to supper and a late night movie. It was actually to impress *her* that just after midnight he looked at the cinema clock and said he was needed at the Embassy!

But now in he came in his big boots, and seeing rats about—no Waterworks employee likes to see rats about—kicked them like so many autumn leaves back into the sewers where they belonged, and then put the man-hole cover back where *it* belonged and fastened it with a great iron bolt, while all the mice took the opportunity to vanish.

That is, all the surviving mice, for they left many dead on the field of action. Fortunately however the corpse of a mere mouse meant nothing

78

to a Waterworks underling, and he left them to lie where they were in their glory until in due course collected by stretcher-bearer parties of the M.P.A.S.

10
The End

THE FUNERAL CEREMONIES for those slain in battle were impressive to a degree. Their graves in the Radish Patch were lined with leaves from the housemaids' now desiccated store, and as Bernard placed above each a single laurel leaf the M.P.A.S. brass band played the Dead March from *Saul,* after which Miss Bianca, in her famous silvery voice, recited an Ode to the Fallen.

ODE TO THE FALLEN, COMPOSED BY MISS BIANCA
ONLY TOO GLAD TO BE ABLE TO
DO SOMETHING AT LAST!

Heroic fellow-mice, how shall we praise ye?

When honor called, not one held back!
Defensive of your happy home the Embassy
How gallantly ye met the rats' attack!

"But oh my poor fatherless little ones!" wept young Mrs. Pickcrumb.

"If only I'd been nicer to my Roly while I had him!" wept old Mrs. Cheesehunter.

"Yet dry your eyes," continued Miss Bianca encouragingly,

> *Shall not fathers and children,*
> *Wives and fond spouses,*
> *Ere long be reunited*
> *In a mouse's*
> *Paradise?*

"I think that's the best poem you've ever written, Miss Bianca," said Bernard afterwards.

"The meter went a bit astray at the end," sighed Miss Bianca, ever the true artist, "but 'twas certainly heartfelt!"

The only incongruous note struck during the proceedings was when Shaun—trust the luck of the Irish!—as the tea-leaves began to prickle popped up *redivivus* (which is Latin for come back to life) he having been not slain after all but only knocked out.

81

The Moot House was put to rights without delay by relays of Scouts and members of the Ladies' Guild. The Scouts went in first, to clean the rude words off the oil painting of the mouse freeing a lion, then the Ladies scrubbed and scrubbed and polished and polished, until all shone like a new pin and formed a worthy setting for the new-hung Roll of Honor.

It was a handsome memorial indeed: the names, in alphabetical order, inscribed in gold nibbled from a cake of gamboge in the Boy's paint-box upon a cedar-wood panel nibbled from one of the Ambassador's discarded cigar-boxes, with surrounding the whole a wreath of imperishable bay fabricated from candle-wax colored green with the Boy's cake of viridian. As has been said, the names were in alphabetical order, but how glad were both Bernard and Miss Bianca that Roly Cheesehunter's stood first!

The Tybalt Star, the M.P.A.S.'s most prized decoration, was awarded all round. (It was actually for gallantry in face of cats, but only one letter, *r* instead of *c*, needed to be changed on the inscription.) However when Miss Bianca suggested that perhaps the Waterworks man deserved one too, Bernard pulled his whiskers.

"But was it not he, after all, who turned the tide of battle in our favor?" argued Miss Bianca—

perhaps remembering her own letter she'd written to the Waterworks Board.

"If he'd come on duty a bit sooner," pointed out Bernard, "there wouldn't have needed to be a battle at all. And you know as well as I do, Miss Bianca, that so long as a single mouse were left alive, never would we have accepted defeat!"

It was true, and Miss Bianca did know it. So long as a single mouse were left alive, the Embassy would have been defended to the last gasp. . . .

"You are right as always, dear Bernard," sighed she. "But what a pity the Ambassador can't know!"

Indeed the Ambassador, returning a few days later with his family and entourage, never knew anything of the great war between the mice and rats, and was actually rather put out to find his box of pen-nibs empty. That rat-blood had encarnadined each one missing, how could he know? He couldn't, as neither could the Ambassadress know that it was only Miss Bianca who had saved the leg of her favorite footstool from being gnawed quite through.

"Dear me, I hope it's not wood-worm!" said she. "See, it's quite rickety! We'll have to find another place for Omar's basket!"

Omar looked as though he thoroughly agreed

with her—for Omar too had naturally returned with the party from the country, and rather to Bernard's and Miss Bianca's indignation never asked a word as to how they had fared after he vamoosed. But it was always his way never to refer to anything disagreeable. . . .

The Boy had of course immediately run up to the schoolroom to see how Miss Bianca was, and to his pleasure (for she'd heard the car coming), found her seated in an easy attitude under a parasol.

"You got your cream cheese all right, while we were away?" asked the Boy. "Thomas Footman looked after you properly?"

With a smile, Miss Bianca gestured towards the empty bonbon dish by her side (kept filled by Bernard amidst all his other duties!), and puffed out a little "ouf!" to show she'd been quite stuffed with cream cheese, so the Boy retained his good opinion of Thomas—though not so the Ambassador, who when he learned from Methuselah how the scamp had simply gone off home, dismissed him without a character and hired another footman in his place, who let us hope proved more trustworthy. Methuselah himself was lucky to escape a similar fate, after the Ambassador discovered how his port had been punished, but was forgiven on account of his great age. As the Ambassadress said, her husband was always too kindhearted!

"And how is your other favorite, Algernon?" asked the Ambassadress, as soon as they were settled down.

"Well, he looks as though he'd been a bit in the wars," said the Boy worriedly. "There's straw sticking out all over his tum. . . ."

"I'll sew it up myself!" promised the Ambassadress—and as next day she did, with a silver needle and silk thread and a golden thimble on her finger, Algernon felt amply rewarded for every wound he'd received in the famous war of the mice against the rats.

It may be said at once that all danger was now past. The underling from the Waterworks Board had well and truly thrust the big bolt back into place over the man-hole, and not a rat ever attempted to get in again. But honor where honor is due, and all honor to the mice in their heroic and successful defense of the Embassy!

It only remains to add that the Boy got a dog after all—not from the Dog Show, but from the Lost Dogs Home, of which the Ambassadress, among all her other good works, was a Lady Patroness, and she killed so to speak two birds with one stone by rejoicing her son and taking at least one puppy off the pay roll. He wasn't nearly as well bred as either Rory or Hamish—a cross, in fact, between a poodle bitch and sire unknown— but very intelligent and affectionate, and the Boy named him Tinker just as planned. His gentle manners with ladies (inherited from his mother), endeared him to Miss Bianca at once, while his gameness in face of any danger (inherited from sire unknown), gave Bernard a good opinion of him too, and thus they all settled down together in peace and friendship, of which both Bernard and Miss Bianca were glad, having by this time had their fill of excitement!